WORLD

-OF-

EEZOES

AN ILLUSTRATED
FIELD GUIDE

Written by Ian Hookham
Illustrated by Ray Steeves
Edited by Ethan Traverse

Text © 2023 Ian Hookham

Illustrations © 2023 Ray Steeves

Edited by Ethan Traverse &
    Jadon Dick

Published by:

OKANAGAN
PUBLISHING HOUSE

www.OkanaganPublishingHouse.ca

Okanagan Publishing House is an imprint of

Okanagan Publishing Inc.
1024 Lone Pine Court
Kelowna, BC V1P 1M7
www.okanaganpublishinghouse.ca

Printed in the United States of America

1st Edition, April 2023

10   9   8   7   6   5   4   3   2   1

ISBN: 978-1-990389-32-0

Library and Archives Canada Cataloguing in Publication

Title: World of Eezoes : an illustrated field guide / written by Ian Hookham ; illustrated by Ray Steeves ; edited by Ethan Traverse. Names: Hookham, Ian, author. | Steeves, Ray, artist. Description: 1st edition. Identifiers: Canadiana 20230501087 | ISBN 9781990389320 (softcover)Subjects: LCGFT: Comics (Graphic works) Classification: LCC PN6733.H66 W674 2023 | DDC 741.5/971—dc23

CONTENTS

For my Bear, who was with me
for every single step, no matter
how difficult it got.

Welcome to your personal guide on the creatures and spirits of World of Eezoes. You'll come to find your common variety in places like the city. There are creatures wandering the streets, rooting through your garbage or simply looking for a treat. They may also be in your own backyard, tending to your garden, sowing seeds, or even destroying it in search of an easy meal!

Other creatures are elusive and rare, with sightings few and far between. You'd have to travel to the farthest depths of the wilds to find them. They could be ancient beings, wandering far from the human eye, with the ability to harness and utilize powerful energy. Should you choose to look for them, be prepared for the unexpected!

As you gain their trust, you'll find in time some creatures will become your companions. And so, with this book as your guide, explore urban spaces, or mountain trails and discover each creature for yourself. Study their unique personalities and defining traits, make observations and sketches, and record your stories to share with others.

At this point, you may be asking yourself, "What makes these spirits and creatures so different from cats, dogs, or any other mammal that we see commonly exist?" The answer lies within us, and every creature for that matter! It all comes down to the ability to utilize and control our Lewin energy.

Lewin energy exists in all living things. It's been described as the core of our beings. So why is it you've never been able to use or see this energy yourself? That is because Lewin energy can usually only be used by creatures who are sparsely populated. All classifications of plants, animals and people draw upon the same energy as a whole. For example, there are over 8 billion people on the planet, so the Lewin that flows within us is spread thin in between all people. Eezoes, however, are extremely rare. The Lewin they contain is much stronger and they have learned the ability to control it.

Whether a creature can wield Lewin or not, each has talents or abilities that are distinctive and unique. They differ just enough from the common species for us to take special notice of them. This book is only the beginning of what we understand of these fantastic creatures!

EEZOE

Eezoes are thought to be spirits,
or fae of the forest; guardians
who protect the delicate balance
between flora and fauna.
They will rarely reveal
themselves to human
eyes and they live
in the deepest parts
of the wilds.
Should you ever
encounter an Eezoe,
it's said a small food offering
or a shiny trinket may coax them to aid you.

The most mysterious part of the Eezoe would be what is
hidden behind those wood-carved masks, as the face of the
Eezoe is completely unknown to humankind. Eezoes often
carve the expression on their masks in the likeness of their
personalities. The true purpose of the
mask is to intimidate and ward off
potential threats to the forest. Eezoes
have nimble fingers, which allow them to
craft and weave with dexterity. They
love collecting curios to accessorize
their belts with and may also carry
herb or food pouches.

4

Eezoes possess a strong amount of Lewin energy. Their main use of Lewin is to heal the sick or injured creatures of the woods, and nurture struggling plants or trees. This process takes energy from their own spirit.

An Eezoe can never expel too much Lewin energy at once, or this would then risk their life.

While Eezoes don't often resort to it, they can use their Lewin to place curses on beings. Eezoes will only usually curse someone who has disobeyed the laws of the forests, or has intentionally caused harm to it. The curses are said to cause paranoia and hallucinations. It is unknown how long they might last. It's better to err on the side of caution, and always treat the forests, plants and animals with respect. No one has been able to get an actual measurement, but it is estimated Eezoes stand 7 to 10 inches from antler tip to foot.

LUMBER SPIRIT

Lumber Spirits are gentle entities that tend to inhabit bits of sticks and logs. They assemble pieces to form a body, held together and animated by their energy. Also referred to as Woodbots, their bodies can sometimes resemble what looks like a wooden robot.

Lumber Spirits form from the left-over Lewin energy of fallen trees. They float around as orbs of light, then take small branches or log rounds from the tree and assemble it into a

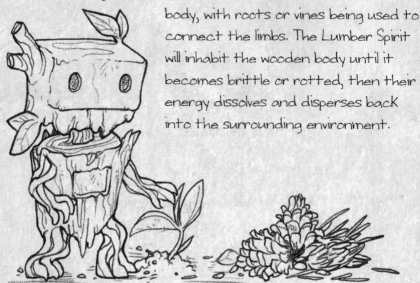

body, with roots or vines being used to connect the limbs. The Lumber Spirit will inhabit the wooden body until it becomes brittle or rotted, then their energy dissolves and disperses back into the surrounding environment.

Lumber Spirits usually don't leave the forest. They are not often seen by people, but have been known to escort lost travelers back to a safe path. Their main purpose is to help scatter the seeds of the fallen tree they were born out of, spreading and growing the forest. Lumber Spirits will pull branches along, filled with seeds, dragging them to parts of the forest that need replanting.

Lumber Spirits usually travel alone, but if there is a particularly bare part of the forest, either from fires or deforestation, they tend to all gather to that spot. Each one bringing seeds from their own trees to mix in with the others. Lumber Spirits don't need to eat or sleep, and will work endlessly to complete their task before their wooden bodies give out.

TIMOUR SPIRIT

A Timour Spirit is an extremely shy entity, also referred to as a house sprite. The theory is that Timour Spirits are a variety of Lumber Spirits that formed in an urban setting, this likely happened while someone was landscaping or removing trees from their property.

While a Lumber Spirit would use the wood from a fallen tree to make their body, a Timour Spirit may not get the same opportunity, with the tree most likely removed and discarded. So Timour Spirits use leftover garbage, such as boxes, bags or cans to create a shell to hide in.

They often wander into people's homes to try and 'help' with houseplants. Sometimes you may find all your indoor plants have been uprooted and replanted outside. It would seem Timour Spirits are confused. Their instincts tell them to spread out in the forest and plant new trees, but the closest they can get is moving around the plants from your home. Have you ever thought about the reason plants and weeds grow in the cracks of sidewalks, or in other seemingly odd places? It could be the Timour Spirit didn't know where else to plant them.

Timour Spirits don't mind being around people, but don't particularly like interacting with them either. If you do encounter a Timour Spirit, it's generally best to ignore its presence and let them be. They can quickly become anxious if they feel cornered or trapped.

GRUMPSHROOM

Grumpshrooms can be found in any moist or rainy habitat. They have a unique ability to communicate with each other at far distances, by connecting their energy to the large underground network of mycelium roots. In the wild, they make their homes in hollow tree logs or under sheltering bushes. They usually live in groups collecting moss, leaves and dried grass to use for their nests. Grumpshrooms also make their homes in people's backyard gardens, especially if it is large, damp and shady.

These pouty little creatures may use their puppy-dog eyes and crocodile tears solely to sucker you out of a snack. They might cry, wail or act as if they are in pain to get your attention. If Grumpshrooms notice people offering treats; watch out! They may swarm you all at once. Grumpshrooms love having the tops of their caps rubbed and will nuzzle people to get affection.

Grumpshrooms can develop in a variety of colour combinations, some variants being very rarely seen. Some people make a hobby of observing Grumpshrooms in different habitats, hoping to find unusual or rare types. They take pictures, record their findings in special journals, and share their photos with online communities.

Grumpshrooms don't need solid food to survive, as they can absorb nutrients from the soil very easily. They simply eat out of pleasure, and will willingly accept most fruit, berries and nuts.

Depending on the variety, fully grown Grumpshrooms can range from as small as 3 inches to as large as 8 inches in height. The ends of their tails also develop differently. Depending on their type, you may see different varieties of leaves and flowers. They use their tails to help them blend in and hide among flowers. As a second defense, they will curl their bodies up as much as possible to hide under their caps.

PUMPKIN IMP

Pumpkin Imps are playful and mischievous little creatures. They are considered the bane of the gardener's existence, and the terror of Halloween Night. While they are not inherently cruel, their pranks and destruction can be seen as such. Pumpkin Imps don't only come out on Halloween, but they are rarely seen during daylight hours. They become a lot more active during the month of October.

Pumpkin Imps burrow deep underground where they live in large warrens. Their tunnels can stretch for miles, right beneath our feet. Pumpkin Imps spend most of the summer and winter down in their burrows, as they don't enjoy the extreme heat or cold. They are most active above ground in the autumn months as it's the perfect temperature for them. Pumpkin Imps have scotopic vision, allowing them to see and move in their dark tunnels and navigate at night.

A Pumpkin Imp has one true love, candy. They will do almost anything to get it, which is why they become such a problem for poor trick or treaters on All Hallows' Eve. They work together as a team. One Pumpkin Imp may vandalize your jack-o'-lantern as a distraction, while the others swipe the bowl of treats! And while they don't intend to harm people, they may push or pull at younger children who seem easy victims for a candy heist.

Pumpkin Imps usually stand 1 to 2 feet high from ear to foot. They walk mainly on two feet but will get down on all fours to make a quick getaway. Their faces are smooth, with the appearance of a gourd. It is thought they evolved this way as a means of camouflage, for if they close their eyes and mouth, they can blend right into a veggie garden. They also enjoy raiding these at night while people are fast asleep.

ICE IMP

Ice Imps are the opposite of Pumpkin Imps. These calm, gentle creatures absolutely love a snowy day, and it's even better if the kids come out to play! Ice Imps can get very attached to children and will watch over and protect them while they are playing out in the snow. Ice Imps will form a sort of pack with people, but when it's time to return home, they are solitary creatures usually living in their caves alone.

While Ice Imps love people, they generally don't enjoy being in their houses, which overheat very quickly. Most live in the forests that edge the cities or out in the countryside. They make homes in rocky caves, using tree boughs for their beds. When they sleep, they roll up into a ball and tuck their arms and legs inside their thick, bushy mane. They also use this method as a means of self-defense if they feel threatened.

In the summertime, Ice Imps will migrate far up north or into places where they can stay cool. You know winter is on its way when the Ice Imps start coming down from the mountains. If you don't see an Ice Imp, you may hear them. They call out to each other in a sort of gurgling yodel. It is theorized that this is a sort of song, though most people consider it no more than a racket. Even so, it's hard to be irritated by a creature so sweet. They enjoy partaking in almost any winter activity. Ice Imps also can harness small amounts of Lewin to control the snow and ice around them, often to the enjoyment of children.

Ice Imps can grow up to 3 feet tall and are a lot heavier than they look. This helps them plow through deep snow and stay grounded on slippery ice. Ice Imps spend most of the autumn storing food in their caves, gathering berries, roots and acorns. They also receive plenty of treats from children, so they never go hungry.

SKRITTLE

Very small, gentle and fluffy, Skrittles can usually be found in the woods. They are mainly nocturnal and hide far up in the sheltering branches of trees, clinging close to the trunk for warmth and stability. They travel in small packs, and on windy nights cling together in pairs, drifting through the air.

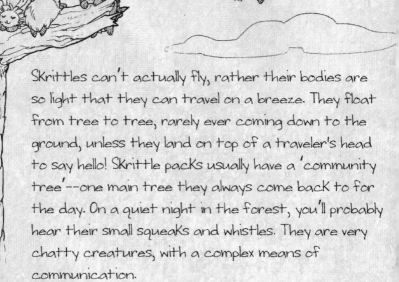

Skrittles can't actually fly, rather their bodies are so light that they can travel on a breeze. They float from tree to tree, rarely ever coming down to the ground, unless they land on top of a traveler's head to say hello! Skrittle packs usually have a 'community tree'--one main tree they always come back to for the day. On a quiet night in the forest, you'll probably hear their small squeaks and whistles. They are very chatty creatures, with a complex means of communication.

Skrittles seem to be particularly attracted to the moon. On cloudless nights, they'll remain active right until sunrise, floating for hours in the air. It is unclear why their connection is so strong, but they will perform a fascinating dance together in a trance like fashion, never breaking their eye contact with the moon. On overcast nights however, they won't travel far from their community tree. When it is time to sleep, they pack themselves all together around the trunk to form one giant fluff ball, sometimes made up of hundreds of Skrittles.

Skrittles generally don't grow much past the size of a dandelion puff, with their fur making up most of their mass. They eat the moss and lichen off tree branches, as well as any nuts or seeds they can find.

PUPBEE

Pupbees are very sweet natured, but they tend to be erratic and hyper. They can become extremely affectionate with people and will even live with them as pets. They embody the personality of dogs, and the instincts of a bee, however their little wings are sufficient only to hover a couple inches off the ground.

When Keeping Pupbees at home, it's important to have at least two or three together. Pupbees are used to thriving in a hive with up to 20 others and they rely on each other for grooming, socializing and companionship. Some people build small nests inside their homes, providing spots to drink nectar from and places to perch. Remember to build the perches low so the Pupbees can reach them, as they also aren't the best climbers!

Since Pupbees are much larger than an actual bumble bee, their nests usually take over the entire base of a tree, fallen logs or small caves. They use sticks and twigs held together by thick dried mud to create their nests, making small pockets or combs to store honey in. There is usually a main chamber to the nest, where all the Pupbees gather at night to sleep in a large pile, keeping each other warm. They don't fully hibernate during the winter, but they do become very lethargic, sleeping most of the time to conserve energy while food may be in short supply.

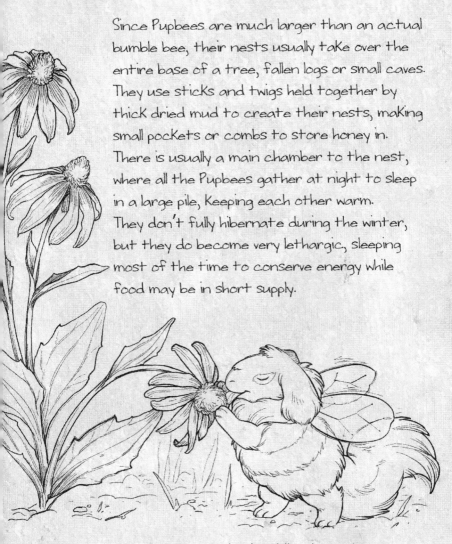

Pupbees are small but can range in size. Like dogs, they can have a variety of different style ears and tails, but for the most part their bodies remain with the classic black and yellow stripes. Monochrome or different shades of yellow or orange colouring has been observed. Like bees, much of their diet relies on the honey they create from the pollen of flowers, but they will also nibble at fruits and berries. They would also gladly accept small biscuits or baked goods.

DEVLING

Devlings are skittish little creatures on their own, but in large hoards they can be quite troublesome. Some people see Devlings as vermin, as they will often rummage through trash cans, spreading garbage around. They also crawl under houses or into attics and make little garbage piles to sleep in, often tearing apart people's belongings to add to their nests.

Devlings have many different colours and patterns on their bodies, with large, hard scales running down the length of their backs. As new scales begin to grow underneath, the old ones will get pushed off and shed. Sometimes this reveals new patterns or colours underneath. On rare occasions, Devlings will develop an iridescence to their scales, which sparkles beautifully and is considered a lucky find.

Devlings eat a wide range of food and will often horde it in their nests. You might have a Devling infestation if the smell of rotting food comes up through your floorboards. In these situations, it is best to contact specially trained professionals. Trying to deal with it on your own could pit you against a whole hoard of angry Devlings. They will use their long tails to lash out, the point of which is very hard and sharp. If cornered or in a desperate situation, Devlings have small mineral pockets at the backs of their jaws and can produce sparks of fire or plumes of smoke to hide in. This tactic is limited though, as it takes a lot of energy out of them.

Devlings can grow up to 2 feet long and prefer a warmer climate. They can be found in most locations, especially closer to areas with large cities. They mainly run on all fours but can walk briefly up on two legs to be able to use their hands to grab at things.

CARECROW

Carecrows are a type of a very squishy, flightless bird. It is speculated that they evolved from the Lewin essence of crows, with a strong desire to be human. Unfortunately, they didn't manage to evolve very far. They are usually described as the epitome of dense, though this description is not intended to be cruel. For what they lack in intelligence, they make up for with their extremely big hearts.

Crows are well known for their intelligence, but it would seem the Carecrow put most of its energy into forming the body they toddle around in, not leaving very much left to form a thought. They do know one thing, that they love being around people! Carecrows often try their best to insert themselves into people's lives, though not everyone has the required patience to manage such a creature.

Carecrows love dressing up in people's clothes. They will steal clothing left out unintentionally to dry on lines, or may even wander into your home and ruffle through your closet. They especially love hats, the sillier the better! To stop the Carecrow from taking their clothes, some people even leave out little outfits out for them to find. Be careful how much attention you give a Carecrow, as they will immediately become attached and follow you almost everywhere.

The one other thing a Carecrow loves almost as equally as people is corn. They'll bumble into corn fields and eat so much they can't move for days. Farmers often have to check their fields before harvesting to make sure there are no roly-poly Carecrows asleep on the ground. Carecrows range in size, with most being between 2 to 3 ft tall, and usually are rather wide.

Zzz

As you have read, the world is filled with many spectacular beings. This is just the beginning, as there are many more creatures out there, in all the different climates and regions. They are in the sea, lakes and rivers, or soaring the skies high above mountain ranges. They wander the land, deep in the wilds or in the tangles of thick jungles, unknown to people. It can only be our hope to live harmoniously next to any and all we may discover.

And now, with your new knowledge and ability to identify some of these different creatures and spirits, create some notes of your own! It might be fun to start a journal to record any new facts you may discover, jot down your experiences or sketch new varieties you find. Journey safely, respect the land and the creatures on it, and have fun sharing notes with your community!

Notes & sketches:

....
....
....
....
....
....

....
....
....
....
....
....

....

....

....

....

....

....

....

....

....

....

....

....

Our truest gratitude to you, the World of Eezoes Community.
Thank you for supporting the development of this book
and all the creatures within it. Thank you for
encouraging the dream to build this fantasy world.
And thank you for all your kind words along the way.

Special thanks to all the friends and family who were also
always there for us, through every part of the adventure!

About the creators

Ian Hookham- Founder and Creature Creator

Ian, aka Kid, has always had a passion for fantasy and magic! He began the original concept for World of Eezoes in 2019 by making the first Eezoe art doll. Since then, he has continued to grow his skill and style in the dolls, as well as develop an abundance of creatures and lore that all fit together. While Ian insists he can't draw, he does doodle out the original character concepts before handing them off to Ray.

Ray Steeves- Illustrator and Designer

Ray is a comic creator and illustrator who is fascinated by naturalism and folklore stories. They design and create many original creatures, comics, characters and graphic arts. They began illustrating for World of Eezoes very early in the project development. With their vast experience in art, Ray often provides creative feedback and ideas when it comes to the character designs.

Ethan Traverse- Office Manager and Creative Assistant

Ethan is a nerd enthusiast at heart, with a long history of a love for video games. He utilizes his experience as an office manager to keep the numbers on track. He recently began assisting in developing the narrative and creature designs, as well as the concepts for the games. Ethan has a creative streak for story-telling and helps to keep the lore consistent.

Thank-you for
Loving the Eezoes!
-Kid

In loving memory of Pudge & Boogie

During the creation of this book, we collectively lost
two beloved family members. Ian and Ethan's dog,
Pudge, and Ray's cat, Boogie, both crossed the
rainbow bridge in 2023. This sketch started out as a
way for us to sneak our pets into the book, but it
became an extremely precious drawing that will
memorialize them forever.

Bonus sketches!

Kid apologizes to all Pupbees for this nightmare sketch!

These are the original sketches Kid sent to Ray for the cover design. As you can see, they had quite the transformation for the final cover!

Manufactured by Amazon.ca
Bolton, ON

34827938R00028